Mee-Ling and the Dragon

A Division of The McGraw-Hill Companies

Columbus, Ohio

www.sra4kids.com

SRA/McGraw-Hill

A Division of The McGraw·Hill Companies

Send all inquiries to:
SRA/McGraw-Hill
8787 Orion Place
Columbus, OH 43240-4027

ISBN 0-07-569948-6
 2 3 4 5 6 7 8 9 DBH 05 04 03 02

A Dry, Dry Land

Once upon a time, in a land far away, there lived a girl named Mee-Ling. She lived with her mother and her father, who were very poor. Indeed, the whole town was very poor. It had not rained in a long time. The land was dry. The crops drooped in the dry, dry soil.

And that was not all. The town lived in fear
of a huge dragon who lived at the top of the
mountain. The dragon breathed smoky flames
and made fearful sounds. Mothers and fathers
told their children, "Never go near the dragon!"

Now, one day, when Mee-Ling's birthday was
drawing near, her mother and father said to her,
"Poor as we are, we wish you to have a fine, big
party. You may ask anyone you please."

Mee-Ling said, "I'll ask all my family and friends, and I will ask the dragon, too!" And she ran out of the house and started up the mountain.

"Come back, foolish girl!" her mother hollered. "The dragon will eat you!"

But Mee-Ling did not care. She went part way
up the mountain. She could hear the dragon
bellowing a fearful song.

"Alone I live, alone I roar!
I am a dragon evermore!"

Mee-Ling ran back down to her house in fear.
"I hope you have learned your lesson," said
her father.

The next day, Mee-Ling's mother said, "Your
birthday list is almost complete. Is there
anyone else you wish to add?"

"I wish to add the dragon," said Mee-Ling,
and she started up the mountain.

"Come back, silly girl!" hollered her father.
"The dragon will knock you over with his
thumping, bumping tail!"

But Mee-Ling did not care. Again she went up the mountain. This time she went farther, until she could see the huge dragon as he bellowed his song.

"Alone I live, alone I cry.
Friendless and sad until I die."

Red-hot stones shot from the dragon's mouth. Mee-Ling turned and ran back home.
"I hope you've learned your lesson," said her mother.

Now it was Mee-Ling's birthday, and all was
ready for her party.

"Poor as we are, your friends and family
have a few small gifts for you on this day. A
little rice from the dry soil, a few seeds from
the dry trees. Is there anything else you wish
for your birthday?" Mee-Ling's mother asked.

"Yes, I wish to ask the dragon to my party," Mee-Ling said, and she started up the mountain.

Her parents called her back. Her friends begged her, "Go no farther!"

But on Mee-Ling went, until she reached the top of the mountain.

At the Top

The rocks and trees shook with the dragon's song, and from his throat came dry, hot dust.

"Alone I live. Who dares come near?
Who can break this curse of fear?"

Mee-Ling was very scared, and she was about to run down the mountain, like all the other times. Then, the fear was replaced with another feeling. She began to feel pity for the lonely dragon. So, she gathered all the courage she could and spoke in the bravest voice she could. "You are indeed a fearful beast. But I have come to invite you to my party," she said.

The dragon stopped roaring.

"Never before in all my life has anyone
dared to speak to me," he said. "You are indeed
a brave child, and a kind one, too! Get up on
my back, Mee-Ling, and we shall go to your
party together."

Mee-Ling got up on the dragon's back, and the dragon began making his way down the mountain. Behind him, his long, blue tail cut a path through the dry, rocky ground.

And as the dragon and Mee-Ling walked down the mountain, a cool and deep blue river began to flow after them. The dragon and Mee-Ling drifted on it into the town.

14